Shadows of the

(A Wallace-A

Spy-Thriller)
Walter Wayne

Shadows Of The Lost Empire

The Wallace-Adhikary Spy-Thrillers, Volume 9

Walter Wayne

Published by Walter Wayne, 2024.

This is a work of fiction. Similarities to real people, places, or events are entirely coincidental.

SHADOWS OF THE LOST EMPIRE

First edition. July 21, 2024.

Written by Walter Wayne.

Also by Walter Wayne

The Scotland Yard Cases
Investigating Alone

The Wallace-Adhikary Spy-Thrillers
The Impenetrable Nexus
Treasure of the Jamaican Buccaneers
Diamonds Aren't Forever
Diamonds In The Shadow
Blood Diamonds
Double Crossed
The Mafia Chronicles
Conspiracy of Chaos
Shadows Of The Lost Empire

As always, thanks to my wife (Krishna) and my son (Chandramouli) without who I wouldn't have been able to write these pieces. Thanks also to those who have encouraged me to keep writing. Aclnowledgements for you, the reader. And finally, my humble thanks to God as well.

The Stolen Relic

Rupert Wallace stood at the edge of the windswept cliff, his gaze fixed on the churning sea below. The salty breeze whipped through his hair as he scanned the horizon, his mind racing with thoughts of the cryptic message he had received from MI6 just hours before.

"The Object has been stolen," the message had read, its words sending a shiver down Rupert's spine. He knew immediately that this was no ordinary theft. The Object was a relic of immense value, a treasure coveted by nations and shadowy organizations alike.

As he stood there, lost in thought, his phone buzzed in his pocket, jolting him back to reality. With a practiced motion, he retrieved the device and glanced at the screen. It was a text from his old friend and fellow operative, Chand Adhikary.

"Rupert, meet me at our usual spot. Urgent."

Rupert's heart raced as he read the message. If Chand was reaching out to him, then the situation was even more dire than he had feared. Without hesitation, he pocketed his phone and turned to leave, his mind already racing with plans and possibilities.

Minutes later, Rupert found himself seated in the dimly lit corner of a quaint little café, his eyes scanning the room for any sign of Chand. It wasn't long before his friend appeared, slipping into the seat across from him with a sense of urgency.

"Rupert, we've got a problem," Chand began, his voice low and urgent. "The Object has been stolen."

Rupert's blood ran cold at the words. He had feared as much, but hearing it confirmed by Chand sent a jolt of adrenaline coursing through his veins. Without a word, he reached into his pocket and retrieved the cryptic message from MI6, sliding it across the table to Chand.

Chand's brow furrowed as he read the message, his mind already racing with possibilities. "This is bad, Rupert. Really bad."

Rupert nodded grimly, his jaw set with determination. "We need to move fast. If the Object has fallen into the wrong hands, it could mean disaster for us all."

Chand nodded in agreement, his eyes alight with a fierce determination. "Agreed. We'll need to mobilize the team and start tracking down leads immediately."

With that, the two friends rose from their seats, their minds already racing with plans and strategies. The Object may have been stolen, but Rupert Wallace and the Adhikary family were not about to let it slip away without a fight.

As they stepped out into the bustling streets of London, Rupert felt a surge of adrenaline course through his veins. The chase was on, and nothing was going to stand in their way.

The Betrayal

The air in the dimly lit alleyway hung heavy with the scent of betrayal as Barry Warner stumbled forward, his breath coming in ragged gasps. Blood dripped from a gash on his forehead, his clothes torn and stained with dirt. He glanced over his shoulder, the sound of footsteps echoing in the empty street behind him.

With a curse, Barry quickened his pace, his mind racing with fear and desperation. He had known the risks when he had agreed to steal the Object for Ms. Gilbert and her criminal organization, El Marciano. But he had never anticipated the depths of her treachery.

As he rounded a corner, Barry's foot caught on a loose cobblestone, sending him sprawling to the ground with a grunt of pain. He scrambled to his feet, his heart pounding in his chest as he pressed on, the echoes of his pursuers growing louder with each passing moment.

Suddenly, a hand closed around Barry's arm, pulling him into the shadows of a nearby alley. He whirled around, his breath catching in his throat as he found himself face to face with a familiar figure.

"Rupert," Barry gasped, relief flooding through him as he recognized his old friend and fellow operative from MI6. "Thank God you're here."

Rupert Wallace's expression was grim as he surveyed Barry's battered form, his eyes narrowing with concern. "What happened, Barry? And where is the Object?"

Barry's gaze flickered with guilt as he recounted the events that had led to his desperate flight through the streets of London. He had been tasked with stealing the Object from a secure vault in the heart of the city, but when he had attempted to deliver it to Ms. Gilbert, she had turned on him, revealing her true intentions.

"She never intended to pay me," Barry confessed, his voice trembling with anger and betrayal. "She double-crossed me and tried to have me killed. I barely managed to escape with my life."

Rupert's jaw tightened with anger as he listened to Barry's tale, his mind racing with possibilities. If Ms. Gilbert had betrayed Barry, then she must have the Object in her possession. And if that was the case, then they needed to act fast before she could unleash its power on the world.

"Barry, you need to tell me everything you know," Rupert said, his voice steely with determination. "Every detail, no matter how small, could be the key to stopping Ms. Gilbert and retrieving the Object."

Barry nodded, his expression grave as he began to recount the clues he had uncovered during his time working for El Marciano. He spoke of secret meetings in darkened alleyways, coded messages exchanged in the dead of night, and whispered rumors of an ancient artifact with the power to reshape the world.

As he listened, Rupert felt a sense of urgency wash over him. Time was running out, and they needed to act fast if they were to have any hope of stopping Ms. Gilbert and recovering the Object before it was too late.

"Barry, you've done well," Rupert said, clapping his friend on the shoulder with a sense of pride. "Now, let's get you somewhere safe and then we'll start putting together a plan of action."

With that, the two men set off into the night, their minds already racing with plans and strategies. The betrayal of Barry Warner had set off a chain reaction of events, but Rupert Wallace was determined to see it through to the end. And if it meant facing off against Ms. Gilbert and her criminal empire, then so be it.

As Rupert and Barry navigated the labyrinthine streets of London, they remained vigilant, their senses on high alert for any sign of danger.

They moved swiftly, taking care to stick to the shadows and avoid drawing attention to themselves.

Finally, they reached a safe house tucked away in a quiet corner of the city. Rupert ushered Barry inside, his eyes scanning the dimly lit interior for any signs of trouble. Satisfied that they were alone, he turned to his friend with a determined expression.

"Barry, you'll be safe here for now," Rupert said, his voice firm. "Rest up and gather your strength. We have a lot of work to do."

Barry nodded gratefully, sinking into a chair with a weary sigh. He knew that he owed Rupert a debt of gratitude for coming to his aid, and he was determined to repay that debt by helping him retrieve the Object and put an end to Ms. Gilbert's plans once and for all.

As Barry settled in for some much-needed rest, Rupert set to work on his laptop, scouring through databases and intelligence reports for any information that could help them track down Ms. Gilbert and the Object. The hours passed in a blur as they worked tirelessly, piecing together clues and formulating a plan of action.

Finally, as the first light of dawn began to creep through the curtains, Rupert leaned back in his chair with a satisfied nod. They had a lead – a rumored meeting between Ms. Gilbert and her associates at a secluded warehouse on the outskirts of the city.

"Barry, it's time," Rupert said, rising to his feet with a sense of purpose. "We need to move fast if we're going to catch them off guard."

Barry nodded, his resolve firm as he followed Rupert out into the cool morning air. They hailed a cab and sped through the empty streets, their hearts pounding with anticipation as they drew closer to their destination.

As they approached the warehouse, Rupert's phone buzzed with a text message. It was Chand, their old friend and fellow operative, reaching out with urgent news.

"Rupert, I've uncovered something big," the message read. "Meet me at our usual spot. We need to talk."

Rupert's brow furrowed with concern as he read the message. Whatever Chand had uncovered, it could be the key to stopping Ms. Gilbert and retrieving the Object. Without hesitation, he directed the cab to change course, setting off on a new path that would lead them straight into the heart of danger.

As they sped through the streets of London, Rupert couldn't shake the feeling that they were racing against time. The betrayal of Barry Warner had set off a chain reaction of events, but with the help of Chand and the rest of the team, they were determined to see it through to the end.

The fate of the world hung in the balance, and Rupert Wallace was ready to face whatever challenges lay ahead. With the Object in their sights and their enemies closing in, they would stop at nothing to ensure that justice was served and the world was safe once more.

The Unraveling

In the sprawling library of the Adhikary family's opulent home in South Kolkata, Dr. Geet Adhikary sat hunched over a dusty tome, his brow furrowed in concentration. Before him lay a collection of cryptic clues provided by Barry Warner, each one a tantalizing piece of a puzzle that promised to unlock the mystery of the stolen Object.

As Dr. Geet meticulously analyzed the clues, his wife, Professor Bulbul, hovered nearby, her sharp eyes scanning the pages of ancient manuscripts for any additional insights. Their son, Detective Chand, paced restlessly, his mind already racing ahead to the next stage of their investigation.

"Father, any progress?" Chand asked, unable to contain his impatience any longer.

Dr. Geet looked up from his work, a gleam of excitement in his eyes. "Yes, Chand, I believe we're onto something. These clues, they're not just random fragments of information. They're part of a larger puzzle, one that stretches back through centuries of history."

Chand's eyes widened with anticipation as Dr. Geet began to piece together the connections between the clues. It was like watching a master craftsman at work, each revelation a stroke of brilliance that illuminated the hidden truths buried within the ancient texts.

"As I suspected, these clues lead us to a series of ancient artifacts scattered across the globe," Dr. Geet explained, his voice filled with awe and wonder. "Each one is a key to unlocking a different aspect of the Object's power."

Professor Bulbul nodded in agreement, her fingers flying across the keyboard of her laptop as she cross-referenced the clues with her extensive knowledge of ancient languages and cultures. Together, they were a formidable team, their collective expertise unrivaled in the world of historical investigation.

As they delved deeper into the mysteries of the Object, they uncovered a web of intrigue that spanned continents and centuries. From the ancient ruins of Mesopotamia to the hidden chambers of the Egyptian pyramids, they followed the trail of clues, piecing together the secrets of the past in their quest to uncover the truth.

But their progress was not without obstacles. Along the way, they encountered numerous adversaries, each one determined to thwart their efforts and claim the Object for themselves. From shadowy operatives lurking in the shadows to powerful figures with their own agendas, the Adhikary family faced danger at every turn.

Yet, they pressed on undeterred, fueled by their determination to uncover the truth and bring the perpetrators to justice. With each new discovery, they grew closer to unraveling the mystery of the Object and unlocking its true power.

Finally, after weeks of tireless effort, they reached a breakthrough. A series of clues led them to a remote monastery nestled high in the mountains of Tibet, where they uncovered the final piece of the puzzle – the key to unlocking the Object's true potential.

As they stood before the ancient artifact, bathed in its otherworldly glow, Dr. Geet felt a sense of awe wash over him. It was a moment of triumph, the culmination of months of hard work and perseverance.

But their victory was short-lived. As they prepared to leave the monastery, they were ambushed by a group of masked assailants, their faces hidden behind dark hoods. With a cry of alarm, Chand leapt into action, his fists flying as he fought to protect his family.

In the chaos that followed, Dr. Geet felt a sharp pain shoot through his side as he was struck by a blow from one of the attackers. With a grunt of pain, he stumbled backwards, his vision swimming as darkness closed in around him.

But even as he fell, he knew that their quest was far from over. The Object may have been within their grasp, but their enemies would stop at nothing to claim it for themselves. And as long as the Adhikary family stood united, they would never give up the fight.

Gasping for breath, Dr. Geet Adhikary fought against the encroaching darkness, his mind reeling with the urgency of their situation. Despite the pain pulsating through his body, he knew that they couldn't afford to falter now. The Object's power was too great, its potential consequences too dire to contemplate if it fell into the wrong hands.

With a determined effort, Dr. Geet forced himself to his feet, his senses sharp as he assessed the situation. Around him, his family fought valiantly against their attackers, their movements a blur of speed and precision.

Detective Chand Adhikary, his son, moved with the grace and agility of a trained martial artist, his fists a blur as he dispatched their assailants with expert precision. Meanwhile, Professor Bulbul Adhikary, his wife, stood her ground with unwavering resolve, her knowledge of ancient languages and cultures proving to be a formidable weapon against their foes.

Drawing upon reserves of strength he didn't know he possessed, Dr. Geet joined the fray, his mind racing with strategies and tactics honed over years of scholarly pursuit and adventurous exploits. Together, they fought as one, a unified force against the tide of darkness threatening to engulf them.

But even as they gained the upper hand, their enemies proved to be relentless in their pursuit. Wave after wave of attackers descended upon them, their numbers seemingly endless as they sought to overwhelm the Adhikary family and claim the Object for themselves.

Amidst the chaos, Dr. Geet caught sight of a figure lurking in the shadows, a glint of malice gleaming in their eyes. It was Ms. Gilbert, the mastermind behind the theft of the Object and the orchestrator of their current predicament.

With a growl of anger, Dr. Geet lunged forward, his fists flying as he sought to confront their adversary head-on. But Ms. Gilbert was no ordinary opponent – she was a skilled combatant, her movements fluid and precise as she deftly parried his blows and countered with lightning-fast strikes of her own.

As the battle raged on, Dr. Geet felt a surge of adrenaline coursing through his veins, his determination to protect his family and retrieve the Object lending him strength in the face of overwhelming odds. With each blow exchanged, each strike landed, he drew closer to victory, his resolve unshakable even in the face of certain death.

Finally, after what felt like an eternity, their adversaries began to falter, their ranks thinning as the Adhikary family fought with unmatched ferocity and determination. With a final, decisive blow, Dr. Geet delivered the finishing blow to Ms. Gilbert, sending her sprawling to the ground with a cry of defeat.

As the dust settled and the echoes of battle faded into silence, Dr. Geet stood victorious, his family at his side, battered but unbroken. The Object was within their grasp once more, its power a testament to their courage and resilience in the face of adversity.

With a sense of grim satisfaction, Dr. Geet turned to his family, a steely determination burning in his eyes. Their journey was far from over, but as long as they stood united, they would overcome any challenge that stood in their way. And together, they would ensure that the Object remained safe from those who sought to wield its power for their own nefarious purposes.

Shadows in Tangier

The labyrinthine streets of Tangier were alive with the hustle and bustle of everyday life, but beneath the surface, a deadly game was about to unfold. As the Adhikary family stepped out of the bustling market square and into the maze-like alleyways of the ancient city, they knew that danger lurked around every corner.

Dr. Geet Adhikary led the way, his eyes scanning the crowded streets for any sign of their adversaries. Beside him, Detective Chand Adhikary walked with a purposeful stride, his hand resting on the hilt of his concealed weapon. Professor Bulbul Adhikary followed close behind, her senses alert for any hint of danger.

As they navigated the narrow alleyways, they could feel the eyes of unseen watchers upon them, their presence like a shadow lingering at the edge of their awareness. They were being hunted, but the Adhikary family was no stranger to danger, and they were more than capable of holding their own against any foe.

Suddenly, a figure emerged from the shadows, blocking their path with a menacing grin. It was one of Ms. Gilbert's operatives, his eyes gleaming with malice as he brandished a wicked-looking blade.

"Going somewhere, Adhikary?" the operative sneered, his voice dripping with contempt. "You're not getting out of Tangier alive."

Without hesitation, Detective Chand sprang into action, his movements a blur of speed as he disarmed the operative with practiced ease. With a swift kick to the chest, he sent the assailant sprawling to the ground, incapacitated but not defeated.

As the Adhikary family pressed on, they encountered more of Ms. Gilbert's operatives at every turn, each one more determined than the last to stop them in their tracks. But the Adhikarys were no ordinary opponents – they were a force to be reckoned with, their skills honed through years of training and experience.

With each confrontation, the Adhikarys fought with unmatched ferocity and determination, their teamwork seamless and their resolve unshakable. But as the battle raged on, they could sense that their adversaries were growing more desperate, their tactics becoming increasingly reckless as they sought to gain the upper hand.

Amidst the chaos, Dr. Geet caught sight of a familiar face in the crowd – it was Barry Warner, their old friend and ally, his eyes wide with fear as he gestured frantically for them to follow him. Without hesitation, the Adhikarys followed Barry through the twisting alleyways, their hearts pounding with anticipation as they raced against time to reach safety.

Finally, they arrived at a secluded courtyard hidden away from prying eyes, their breath coming in ragged gasps as they caught their breath. Barry wasted no time in explaining the situation – Ms. Gilbert had set a trap for them, luring them into Tangier with the promise of information about the Object's whereabouts.

"We need to move fast," Barry urged, his voice urgent. "Ms. Gilbert's operatives are closing in, and we're running out of time."

With a nod of agreement, Dr. Geet turned to his family, his expression grim. "We can't let Ms. Gilbert get her hands on the Object. We need to find it before she does, no matter what it takes."

Determined to stay one step ahead of their enemies, the Adhikary family set out once more into the labyrinthine streets of Tangier, their senses sharp and their resolve unyielding. With danger lurking around every corner, they knew that the hunt for the Object had only just begun – and the stakes had never been higher.

As the Adhikary family continued their pursuit through the maze-like streets of Tangier, the sense of urgency weighed heavily upon them. They knew they were on a race against time, with Ms. Gilbert's operatives hot on their trail and the fate of the Object hanging in the balance.

Their footsteps echoed against the ancient walls as they weaved through the narrow alleyways, their senses alert for any sign of danger. Detective Chand took point, his keen instincts guiding them through the labyrinth of streets as they dodged obstacles and evaded pursuit.

Suddenly, a shadowy figure darted out from a darkened doorway, blocking their path with a menacing sneer. It was one of Ms. Gilbert's elite enforcers, a formidable opponent armed with lethal precision and unwavering determination.

Without hesitation, Chand sprang into action, his movements fluid and precise as he engaged the enforcer in a fierce hand-to-hand combat. Meanwhile, Dr. Geet and Professor Bulbul stood their ground, ready to provide support as needed.

The clash of steel rang out through the alleyway as Chand and the enforcer traded blows, their movements a blur of speed and skill. Despite the enforcer's formidable prowess, Chand's determination and training proved to be a match for their adversary, and with a decisive strike, he disarmed the enforcer and rendered them incapacitated.

With the immediate threat neutralized, the Adhikary family pressed on, their hearts pounding with adrenaline as they continued their search for the Object. They knew they were closing in, their instincts leading them ever closer to their elusive quarry.

But as they turned a corner into a deserted courtyard, they were suddenly confronted by a scene of chaos. Ms. Gilbert's operatives had set a trap, surrounding them on all sides with nowhere to run.

"We've walked right into their hands," Professor Bulbul exclaimed, her voice tinged with frustration as she surveyed their surroundings.

Dr. Geet's jaw tightened with determination as he assessed the situation, his mind racing with possibilities. They were outnumbered and outgunned, but they couldn't afford to back down now – not when the fate of the world hung in the balance.

"We need to hold them off while we come up with a plan," Dr. Geet said, his voice firm. "Chand, hold the line. Bulbul, see if you can find a way out of here. Barry, stay close and be ready to provide support."

With a nod of agreement, the Adhikary family sprang into action, each member playing their part in the deadly game of cat and mouse unfolding before them. Chand stood at the forefront, his fists flying as he fended off wave after wave of attackers, while Professor Bulbul searched for an escape route amidst the chaos.

Meanwhile, Dr. Geet and Barry worked together to devise a strategy, their minds racing with possibilities as they sought a way to outmaneuver their adversaries. With each passing moment, the tension mounted, the air thick with the sound of clashing steel and the cries of battle.

But just as it seemed that all hope was lost, a sudden commotion erupted from the rooftops above. A group of shadowy figures descended upon their attackers with ruthless efficiency, their movements swift and precise as they turned the tide of battle in the Adhikary family's favor.

With their newfound allies at their side, the Adhikary family fought with renewed vigor, their determination unyielding as they pushed back against their enemies with unmatched ferocity. In the chaos of battle, they glimpsed a fleeting opportunity – a chance to break free from their assailants and continue their pursuit of the Object.

With a final, decisive strike, they broke through the enemy lines and fled into the night, their hearts pounding with adrenaline as they raced towards their next destination. The hunt for the Object had only just begun, but the Adhikary family was more determined than ever to see it through to the end.

Echoes of Marrakesh

Marrakesh, with its vibrant colors and bustling souks, seemed to pulsate with life as the Adhikary family stepped foot into the ancient city. But beneath the surface, hidden within the labyrinthine alleyways and quiet corners of the old city, lay a web of deception waiting to be unraveled.

Dr. Geet Adhikary led the way, his keen eyes scanning the crowded streets for any sign of their next lead. Detective Chand Adhikary followed close behind, his senses on high alert as he surveyed their surroundings for potential threats. Professor Bulbul Adhikary walked beside them, her mind already racing with possibilities as she analyzed the clues they had gathered thus far.

As they navigated the bustling souks, they could feel the weight of their mission pressing down upon them. The Object remained elusive, its whereabouts shrouded in mystery, but they knew that Marrakesh held the key to unlocking its secrets.

Their first stop was a nondescript tea house tucked away in a quiet alleyway, where they hoped to gather information from the locals about any recent sightings or suspicious activity. As they entered the dimly lit interior, they were greeted by the scent of fragrant spices and the murmur of conversation.

Dr. Geet approached the proprietor, a weathered man with a twinkle in his eye and a knowing smile upon his lips. With a practiced charm, he engaged the man in conversation, his words laced with subtle inquiries about the Object and its rumored presence in Marrakesh.

At first, the proprietor seemed reluctant to divulge any information, but as Dr. Geet pressed on, his persistence began to pay off. With a cautious glance over his shoulder, the man leaned in close and whispered a name – Hassan al-Farsi, a notorious smuggler known to frequent the alleys of the old city.

With a nod of thanks, Dr. Geet rejoined his family, a sense of determination burning bright in his eyes. They had their lead, and they wouldn't rest until they had uncovered the truth about the Object and put an end to Ms. Gilbert's plans once and for all.

Their journey took them deeper into the heart of the old city, where the narrow alleyways twisted and turned like a labyrinth, leading them ever closer to their elusive quarry. With each step, they could feel the weight of history pressing down upon them, the echoes of Marrakesh's ancient past reverberating through the cobblestone streets.

But as they neared their destination, they could sense that they were not alone. Shadows lurked in the corners, their movements furtive and elusive as they watched the Adhikary family's every move with keen interest.

Suddenly, a figure emerged from the darkness, blocking their path with a menacing sneer. It was Hassan al-Farsi, the smuggler they had been searching for, his eyes gleaming with malice as he brandished a wicked-looking blade.

"Looking for something, Adhikary?" Hassan taunted, his voice dripping with contempt. "You won't find it here."

Without hesitation, Chand stepped forward, his hand resting on the hilt of his concealed weapon as he faced off against the smuggler. But before either of them could make a move, they were interrupted by a sudden commotion from the rooftops above.

A group of masked figures descended upon them with ruthless efficiency, their movements swift and precise as they engaged Hassan's men in a deadly game of cat and mouse. With the odds stacked against them, the Adhikary family fought with unmatched ferocity, their determination unyielding as they pushed back against their adversaries with everything they had.

In the chaos of battle, Dr. Geet caught sight of a glint of metal lying amidst the rubble – it was the Object, its ancient form glowing with an otherworldly light as it lay abandoned on the ground. With a surge of adrenaline coursing through his veins, he reached out and snatched it up, his fingers tingling with its power.

But before he could react, a sudden explosion rocked the alleyway, sending debris flying in all directions. With a cry of alarm, the Adhikary family was thrown to the ground, their senses reeling as they struggled to regain their bearings.

As the smoke cleared and the dust settled, they found themselves face to face with their adversaries once more, their eyes blazing with determination as they prepared to make their final stand. The hunt for the Object had led them to Marrakesh, but the battle was far from over – and the fate of the world hung in the balance.

With their adversaries closing in, the Adhikary family knew they had to act fast. Dr. Geet clutched the Object tightly in his hand, feeling its power pulsating through his veins. It was now or never.

Detective Chand sprang into action, his movements fluid and precise as he engaged their attackers in a fierce hand-to-hand combat. His fists flew like lightning, delivering powerful blows that sent their adversaries reeling backward.

Meanwhile, Professor Bulbul remained at Dr. Geet's side, her mind racing as she assessed the situation. With a quick glance around, she spotted a narrow alleyway leading off from the main street – a potential escape route.

"Follow me!" she shouted, her voice cutting through the chaos as she led the way into the alley. The rest of the family followed close behind, their footsteps echoing against the ancient walls as they fled from their pursuers.

As they ran, Dr. Geet could feel the Object pulsating with energy in his hand, its power growing stronger with each passing moment. He knew they were getting closer to uncovering its true purpose, but they had to stay one step ahead of Ms. Gilbert's operatives if they were to succeed.

Suddenly, they emerged into a secluded courtyard, the sound of their pursuers fading into the distance behind them. With a sigh of relief, Dr. Geet leaned against the crumbling wall, his heart pounding with adrenaline as he caught his breath.

But their respite was short-lived. Before they could react, a group of masked figures emerged from the shadows, surrounding them on all sides with weapons drawn. It seemed they had walked right into another trap.

"We've got them now," one of the operatives sneered, a wicked grin spreading across their face. "There's nowhere left to run."

But Dr. Geet refused to back down. With a steely determination in his eyes, he raised the Object high above his head, its glow illuminating the courtyard with an otherworldly light.

"Stay back!" he warned, his voice filled with authority. "We won't hesitate to use this if you leave us no choice."

For a moment, the operatives hesitated, their eyes wide with fear and uncertainty. They knew the power of the Object, and they didn't dare risk facing its wrath.

But just as it seemed the standoff would end peacefully, a sudden explosion rocked the courtyard, sending shockwaves rippling through the air. With a cry of alarm, the operatives were thrown off balance, their ranks scattering in disarray.

Amidst the chaos, Dr. Geet caught sight of a familiar face in the crowd – it was Barry Warner, their old friend and ally, his expression grim as he fought his way through the throng of adversaries.

"Come on, we don't have much time," Barry shouted, gesturing for the Adhikary family to follow him. Without hesitation, they followed him through the maze of alleyways, their hearts pounding with adrenaline as they raced against time to escape.

As they fled from their pursuers, Dr. Geet couldn't help but feel a surge of gratitude towards Barry. Despite everything they had been through, he had remained loyal to their cause, risking his own life to ensure their safety.

With Barry's help, they managed to evade their enemies and disappear into the shadows of Marrakesh once more. But as they regrouped in a secluded hideout, Dr. Geet knew that their journey was far from over.

The hunt for the Object had led them to Marrakesh, but they were no closer to uncovering its true purpose. With danger lurking around every corner and their enemies closing in, they would need to stay one step ahead if they were to succeed in their mission and prevent catastrophe from befalling the world.

The High Atlas Gambit

As danger closed in around them, Rupert Wallace and Detective Chand Adhikary found themselves navigating the treacherous terrain of the High Atlas Mountains. With each step, they raced against time, their senses on high alert as they sought to reach the next clue in their quest to uncover the truth about the Object.

The jagged peaks loomed overhead, their snow-capped summits obscured by swirling clouds. The air was thin and biting, a sharp contrast to the sweltering heat of Marrakesh, but Rupert and Chand pressed on undeterred, their determination unyielding in the face of adversity.

With each passing moment, the tension mounted, the silence of the mountains broken only by the sound of their footsteps crunching against the rocky ground. They knew that danger lurked around every corner, but they refused to let fear dictate their actions.

Suddenly, a shout echoed through the crisp mountain air, followed by the sound of gunfire. Without hesitation, Rupert and Chand sprang into action, their instincts guiding them towards the source of the commotion.

As they rounded a bend in the trail, they came upon a group of masked assailants locked in a fierce firefight with a lone figure standing defiantly against the onslaught. It was Barry Warner, their old friend and ally, his back pressed against a sheer cliff face as he fought off their attackers with unmatched skill and determination.

"Barry, we're here to help!" Rupert shouted, his voice carrying over the roar of gunfire. With a nod of acknowledgment, Barry continued to hold his ground, his eyes flashing with determination as he exchanged blows with their adversaries.

With the odds stacked against them, Rupert and Chand sprang into action, their weapons drawn as they joined the fray. With each shot fired and each blow landed, they gained ground against their enemies, driving them back with relentless force.

But even as they fought, the sound of approaching reinforcements echoed through the mountains, their footsteps growing louder with each passing moment. With no time to spare, Rupert knew they had to act fast if they were to reach their next destination and uncover the next clue in their quest.

"Barry, we need to keep moving," Rupert shouted over the din of battle. "We can't stay here."

With a grim nod of agreement, Barry disengaged from the firefight, his eyes scanning the rugged terrain for any sign of a way forward. With a steely determination in his eyes, he led the way, his footsteps sure and confident as he navigated the treacherous mountain pass.

As they ascended higher into the mountains, the air grew thinner and the terrain more unforgiving. With each step, they faced new challenges – sheer cliffs, icy ravines, and hidden pitfalls lying in wait to ensnare the unwary.

But Rupert and Chand pressed on undeterred, their resolve unyielding as they pushed themselves to their limits in their quest to uncover the truth about the Object. With each passing moment, they drew closer to their goal, their determination unshakable even in the face of seemingly insurmountable odds.

Finally, as the sun began to set behind the towering peaks, they reached their destination – a secluded mountain pass hidden away from prying eyes. With a sense of urgency, Rupert and Chand began to search the area, scouring every nook and cranny for any sign of the next clue.

And then, just as they were about to give up hope, Chand spotted something glinting in the fading light – a small, metallic object half-buried in the snow. With a triumphant shout, he reached down and retrieved it, his heart pounding with excitement as he realized what they had found.

It was the next clue, a key piece of the puzzle in their quest to uncover the truth about the Object. With renewed determination, Rupert and Chand set off once more, their spirits buoyed by the knowledge that they were one step closer to their goal.

But as they descended from the mountains and made their way back towards civilization, they knew that their journey was far from over. The Object remained elusive, its true purpose still shrouded in mystery, but they were more determined than ever to see their mission through to the end – no matter what dangers lay ahead.

As Rupert, Chand, and Barry descended from the rugged peaks of the High Atlas Mountains, they knew that their respite would be short-lived. With the next clue in hand, their journey was far from over, and danger still lurked around every corner.

As they made their way back towards civilization, the landscape gradually shifted from the harsh, unforgiving terrain of the mountains to the more hospitable valleys below. But even as they left the treacherous slopes behind, they remained vigilant, their senses attuned to any signs of pursuit.

As they reached the foothills of the mountains, Chand's keen eyes caught sight of a faint glimmer in the distance – the lights of a small village nestled amidst the rolling hills. It was their next destination, and they wasted no time in making their way towards it.

As they entered the village, they were greeted by the warm glow of lanterns and the sounds of laughter echoing through the narrow streets. But beneath the facade of normalcy, Chand could sense an undercurrent of tension in the air, a sense of unease that hung heavy over the village like a shroud.

With the next clue burning a hole in his pocket, Chand wasted no time in seeking out the local inhabitants for information. He approached a group of villagers gathered outside a small tavern, their voices hushed as they spoke in low tones.

"Excuse me," Chand said, his voice cutting through the murmurs of conversation. "We're looking for information about a certain artifact. Have you heard anything that might be of help to us?"

The villagers exchanged nervous glances, their expressions guarded as they eyed Chand and his companions warily. But before they could respond, a figure emerged from the shadows – an elderly woman with a weathered face and piercing eyes that seemed to bore into Chand's soul.

"I may be able to help you," the woman said, her voice soft but commanding. "But first, you must prove yourselves worthy of my trust."

With a nod of agreement, Chand stepped forward, his determination shining bright in his eyes. "What do you need us to do?"

The woman's gaze lingered on Chand for a moment, as if assessing his resolve, before she spoke again. "There is a task that needs to be completed – a test of strength and courage that will prove whether you are worthy of the knowledge you seek."

Without hesitation, Chand accepted the challenge, his heart pounding with anticipation as he prepared to face whatever trials lay ahead. With a solemn nod, the woman led them out of the village and into the surrounding countryside, where a series of obstacles awaited them.

As they made their way through the rugged landscape, they encountered challenges of every kind – from steep cliffs to rushing rivers to dense forests teeming with wildlife. But with each obstacle overcome, Chand felt a sense of exhilaration coursing through his veins, his determination unwavering in the face of adversity.

Finally, after hours of grueling effort, they reached their destination – a secluded clearing deep in the heart of the forest. In the center of the clearing stood a small stone pedestal, upon which rested the next clue in their quest.

With a sense of anticipation, Chand approached the pedestal and retrieved the clue, his heart pounding with excitement as he read the inscription carved into its surface. It was a riddle, a cryptic puzzle that promised to unlock the next step in their journey.

As he pondered the riddle, Chand felt a surge of determination coursing through his veins. They were one step closer to uncovering the truth about the Object, and nothing would stand in their way.

With the next clue in hand, Chand turned to his companions, a determined glint in his eyes. "Let's go," he said, his voice ringing with conviction. "We have a mystery to solve, and time is of the essence."

And with that, they set off once more, their spirits buoyed by the knowledge that they were closer than ever to uncovering the secrets of the Object and putting an end to Ms. Gilbert's plans once and for all.

Jungle Shadows

The dense canopy of the Amazon jungle stretched out before them like an impenetrable wall, its lush foliage teeming with life and mystery. Rupert Wallace, Detective Chand Adhikary, and Barry Warner forged their way through the thick undergrowth, their senses on high alert as they closed in on the Object's hiding place.

The air was thick with humidity, the oppressive heat weighing down upon them like a suffocating blanket. But despite the sweltering conditions, they pressed on undeterred, their determination unyielding in the face of the challenges that lay ahead.

As they delved deeper into the heart of the jungle, they could sense that they were not alone. Shadows flitted through the underbrush, their movements elusive and mysterious as they watched the intruders' progress with keen interest.

With each step, the tension mounted, the jungle closing in around them like a living, breathing entity. But Rupert, Chand, and Barry remained vigilant, their senses attuned to any signs of danger that lurked in the shadows.

Suddenly, a rustling in the foliage ahead caught their attention, and they froze in their tracks, their eyes scanning the surrounding jungle for any sign of movement. But before they could react, a group of armed mercenaries burst from the undergrowth, their weapons raised and their expressions hostile.

"Stop right there!" one of the mercenaries barked, his voice ringing out through the jungle. "This is private property. You have no business being here."

But Rupert was undeterred. "We're here on official business," he replied, his voice calm but firm. "We're searching for an artifact of great importance, and we won't let anyone stand in our way."

The mercenaries exchanged wary glances, their expressions conflicted as they weighed their options. But before they could make a move, a new figure emerged from the shadows – a woman clad in jungle camouflage, her eyes gleaming with malice as she surveyed the intruders with contempt.

It was Ms. Gilbert, their elusive adversary, and she had no intention of letting them interfere with her plans. "Well, well, well," she sneered, her voice dripping with disdain. "If it isn't the infamous Rupert Wallace and his band of merry adventurers. I must say, I'm impressed by your tenacity. But I'm afraid your journey ends here."

With a wave of her hand, Ms. Gilbert signaled to her mercenaries, and they moved in to surround Rupert, Chand, and Barry. But the Adhikary family was not about to go down without a fight.

With a battle cry, Chand sprang into action, his fists flying as he engaged the mercenaries in a fierce hand-to-hand combat. Meanwhile, Rupert and Barry exchanged gunfire with their adversaries, their weapons blazing as they fought to hold their ground.

But as the battle raged on, it became clear that they were outnumbered and outgunned. The mercenaries pressed in on all sides, their relentless onslaught pushing Rupert, Chand, and Barry to their limits.

Just when it seemed that all hope was lost, a new sound echoed through the jungle – the roar of a wild beast, its powerful presence shaking the ground beneath their feet. With a sense of dread, Rupert and his companions turned to see a massive jaguar emerge from the shadows, its eyes blazing with primal fury as it charged towards them.

But instead of attacking, the jaguar leaped past them with lightning speed, its target not Rupert and his companions, but their adversaries. With a ferocious growl, it pounced upon the mercenaries, its claws and fangs tearing through flesh and bone with savage precision.

As chaos erupted around them, Rupert, Chand, and Barry seized the opportunity to make their escape, ducking into the dense undergrowth as they fled from the scene of battle. Behind them, the sounds of screams and gunfire echoed through the jungle, but they dared not look back – they had a mission to complete, and nothing would stand in their way.

As they forged deeper into the heart of the jungle, the air grew thick with tension, the oppressive weight of the jungle bearing down upon them like a suffocating blanket. But despite the dangers that lurked around every corner, they pressed on undeterred, their resolve unyielding in the face of adversity.

Finally, after what felt like an eternity, they reached their destination – a secluded clearing hidden away from prying eyes. In the center of the clearing stood a massive stone temple, its ancient form looming ominously against the backdrop of the jungle.

With a sense of trepidation, Rupert, Chand, and Barry approached the temple, their hearts pounding with anticipation as they prepared to uncover the secrets that lay within. Little did they know, they were about to confront ancient guardians and unravel the mysteries of the Object's true purpose – but whether they would emerge unscathed from the depths of the jungle remained to be seen.

As they cautiously approached the ancient stone temple, the atmosphere around them seemed to crackle with tension. Vines snaked around the weathered stones, hinting at the passage of centuries since the temple's construction. Rupert, Chand, and Barry exchanged wary glances, their senses on high alert for any signs of danger lurking within.

With a silent nod of agreement, Rupert took the lead, his eyes scanning the intricate carvings adorning the temple walls for any clues or symbols that might offer insight into its mysteries. Chand and Barry followed closely behind, their weapons drawn and their nerves taut with anticipation.

As they reached the towering entrance of the temple, a sense of foreboding washed over them like a tidal wave. The heavy stone doors stood sentinel, their ancient glyphs and symbols whispering secrets of times long past. With a deep breath, Rupert pushed against the doors, the heavy stone groaning in protest as they swung open to reveal the darkness within.

The interior of the temple was shrouded in shadow, the air thick with the scent of must and decay. As they ventured deeper into its depths, they could hear the faint echoes of their footsteps reverberating off the ancient walls, each step a testament to the weight of history that surrounded them.

Suddenly, a flicker of movement caught Rupert's eye, and he froze in his tracks, his senses on high alert. Peering into the darkness ahead, he could make out the outlines of ancient statues lining the walls of the temple, their stone forms watching silently as the intruders approached.

With a sense of unease, Rupert motioned for Chand and Barry to proceed with caution, their footsteps echoing softly against the stone floor as they moved deeper into the temple's depths. As they passed beneath the watchful gaze of the statues, they could feel a palpable sense of tension building in the air, as if the very walls themselves were closing in around them.

Suddenly, a low rumbling echoed through the temple, and the ground beneath their feet began to tremble. With a sense of dread, Rupert and his companions realized that they were not alone – ancient guardians, awakened from their slumber, were rising to defend the temple from intruders.

With a roar, the guardians emerged from the shadows, their massive forms towering over Rupert, Chand, and Barry like titans of old. Carved from stone and imbued with ancient magic, they moved with an otherworldly grace, their eyes glowing with an inner fire as they prepared to strike.

But Rupert was undeterred. Drawing upon his training and experience, he rallied his companions to stand firm against the onslaught, their weapons raised and their resolve unyielding in the face of the guardians' fury.

With a battle cry, Chand charged forward, his fists flying as he engaged the guardians in a fierce hand-to-hand combat. Meanwhile, Rupert and Barry exchanged gunfire with their adversaries, their weapons blazing as they fought to hold their ground against the relentless onslaught.

As the battle raged on, the temple echoed with the clash of steel and the roar of combat, each blow struck a testament to the strength and determination of Rupert, Chand, and Barry. Despite the odds stacked against them, they fought with unmatched ferocity, their spirits unbroken even as the guardians closed in around them.

But just when it seemed that all hope was lost, a blinding light erupted from the depths of the temple, illuminating the chamber with an otherworldly glow. With a sense of awe, Rupert and his companions watched as the ancient guardians were consumed by the light, their stone forms crumbling to dust as they were banished back to the depths from whence they came.

With the guardians defeated, Rupert, Chand, and Barry pressed on, their hearts pounding with excitement as they ventured deeper into the temple's depths. Little did they know, they were about to uncover the final piece of the puzzle – the true purpose of the Object, and the role it would play in shaping the fate of the world.

Machu Picchu's Secret

The ruins of Machu Picchu loomed before them, its ancient stone structures rising majestically against the backdrop of the Andean mountains. Dr. Geet Adhikary, his wife Professor Bulbul, and their son Detective Chand Adhikary stood at the entrance to the ancient city, their hearts pounding with excitement as they prepared to uncover the secrets that lay hidden within.

As they made their way through the winding pathways of the ruins, Dr. Geet's keen eyes scanned the intricate carvings adorning the walls, his mind racing with possibilities as he pieced together the clues that would unlock the mysteries of the Object.

With each step, they delved deeper into the heart of Machu Picchu, their senses attuned to the ancient energy that pulsed through the stone. But as they approached the center of the city, they could sense that they were not alone – a dangerous adversary was lurking in the shadows, watching their every move with keen interest.

Suddenly, a voice rang out from the darkness, its tone dripping with malice and contempt. "Well, well, well," it sneered. "If it isn't the esteemed Dr. Geet Adhikary and his band of meddling adventurers. I must say, I'm impressed by your tenacity. But I'm afraid your journey ends here."

With a sense of dread, Dr. Geet and his companions turned to face their adversary, their eyes narrowing with suspicion as they tried to make out the figure lurking in the shadows. And then, emerging from the darkness, they saw her – Ms. Gilbert, their elusive adversary, her eyes gleaming with malice as she regarded them with contempt.

"Ms. Gilbert," Dr. Geet said, his voice calm but firm. "I should have known you would be behind this. What are you doing here?"

Ms. Gilbert chuckled darkly, her lips curling into a sinister smile. "I'm here for the same reason you are, Dr. Adhikary – to uncover the secrets of the Object and claim its power for myself. But unlike you, I'm not afraid to do whatever it takes to get what I want."

With a wave of her hand, Ms. Gilbert signaled to her minions, and they moved in to surround Dr. Geet and his companions. But the Adhikary family was not about to go down without a fight.

With a battle cry, Chand sprang into action, his fists flying as he engaged Ms. Gilbert's minions in a fierce hand-to-hand combat. Meanwhile, Dr. Geet and Professor Bulbul exchanged knowing glances, their minds racing as they searched for a way to outmaneuver their adversary.

Suddenly, Dr. Geet's eyes lit up with realization as he spotted a series of ancient glyphs carved into the wall of the temple. With a sense of urgency, he motioned for Professor Bulbul to join him, her expertise in ancient languages and history proving invaluable as they deciphered the hidden messages contained within.

As they worked, they uncovered a series of clues that shed light on the true purpose of the Object – a powerful artifact imbued with the ability to control the elements and reshape the world according to the will of its wielder. But with great power came great danger, and they realized that the Object had the potential to bring about untold destruction if it fell into the wrong hands.

With their discovery in hand, Dr. Geet and Professor Bulbul turned to confront Ms. Gilbert, their determination unyielding as they prepared to face their adversary head-on. But before they could make a move, a sudden rumbling echoed through the ruins, shaking the ground beneath their feet.

With a sense of dread, they looked up to see a massive boulder hurtling towards them, its momentum unstoppable as it bore down upon them with terrifying speed. With no time to spare, Dr. Geet and his companions leaped out of the way, narrowly avoiding being crushed beneath the weight of the stone.

As they scrambled to their feet, they realized that Ms. Gilbert had triggered a trap – a deadly booby trap designed to eliminate anyone who dared to challenge her authority. With a sense of urgency, Dr. Geet and his companions made a break for it, their hearts pounding with adrenaline as they raced against time to escape the ruins before it was too late.

With each step, they could feel the ground trembling beneath their feet, the ruins collapsing around them as the ancient city crumbled into dust. But despite the chaos and destruction that surrounded them, they pressed on undeterred, their determination unyielding as they fought to survive against all odds.

Finally, after what felt like an eternity, they emerged from the ruins of Machu Picchu, their bodies bruised and battered but their spirits unbroken. With a sense of relief, they watched from a safe distance as the ancient city collapsed into rubble, its secrets lost to the sands of time once more.

As they caught their breath and took stock of their surroundings, Dr. Geet and his companions knew that their journey was far from over. The Object remained elusive, its true purpose still shrouded in mystery, but they were more determined than ever to see their mission through to the end – no matter what dangers lay ahead.

As they caught their breath and surveyed the aftermath of their narrow escape from Machu Picchu, Dr. Geet Adhikary and his companions knew that their quest was far from over. The Object's true purpose remained a mystery, and the threat posed by Ms. Gilbert and her ruthless pursuit of power loomed large.

With a sense of urgency, Dr. Geet turned to his wife, Professor Bulbul, and their son, Detective Chand, his eyes filled with determination. "We cannot let Ms. Gilbert get her hands on the Object," he said, his voice resolute. "We must do whatever it takes to stop her."

Chand nodded in agreement, his expression grave as he considered the implications of their next move. "But how do we stop her?" he asked, his voice tinged with uncertainty. "She's proven herself to be a formidable adversary, and she won't hesitate to use any means necessary to achieve her goals."

Dr. Geet's mind raced as he pondered Chand's question, his thoughts swirling with possibilities. Suddenly, a spark of inspiration lit up his eyes, and he turned to his companions with newfound resolve.

"We need to find out more about the Object – its origins, its purpose, and how we can neutralize its power," he said, his voice tinged with excitement. "And I know just where to start."

With a sense of purpose, Dr. Geet led his companions away from the ruins of Machu Picchu and back into the heart of the Amazon jungle. Their journey had taken them to some of the most remote and treacherous corners of the world, but they were undeterred in their quest to uncover the truth.

Their destination was a hidden temple deep within the jungle, rumored to hold the key to unlocking the secrets of the Object. With each step, they could feel the ancient energy of the jungle pulsing around them, guiding them towards their destination with an otherworldly force.

Finally, after hours of trekking through the dense undergrowth, they reached their destination – a secluded clearing hidden away from prying eyes. In the center of the clearing stood the temple, its weathered stone walls adorned with intricate carvings and glyphs that spoke of a bygone era.

With a sense of reverence, Dr. Geet led his companions into the temple, their footsteps echoing softly against the ancient stone floor.

As they ventured deeper into its depths, they could feel a sense of awe washing over them, as if they were stepping back in time to a world long forgotten.

Suddenly, they came upon a chamber filled with ancient artifacts and relics, each one more mysterious than the last. But it was the centerpiece of the chamber – a pedestal adorned with the Object itself – that drew their attention.

With a sense of trepidation, Dr. Geet approached the pedestal and reached out to touch the Object, his fingers tingling with anticipation as he made contact with its smooth surface. As he did, a surge of energy coursed through him, filling him with a sense of power and purpose unlike anything he had ever experienced before.

With a newfound sense of clarity, Dr. Geet turned to his companions, his eyes shining with determination. "We must find a way to neutralize the Object's power," he said, his voice filled with conviction. "And I believe that the key lies within these ancient texts and relics."

With that, they set to work, scouring the chamber for any clues or symbols that might offer insight into the Object's true nature. Hours passed as they poured over ancient manuscripts and deciphered cryptic glyphs, their minds racing with possibilities as they pieced together the puzzle of the Object's origins.

And then, just as they were about to give up hope, Dr. Geet stumbled upon a passage in one of the ancient texts – a prophecy that spoke of a chosen one who would wield the power of the Object for the good of mankind.

With a sense of excitement, Dr. Geet shared his discovery with his companions, their spirits buoyed by the possibility of a solution to their dilemma. But their celebration was short-lived, for they knew that their adversary was still out there, lurking in the shadows and waiting for her chance to strike.

With a renewed sense of purpose, Dr. Geet and his companions set out once more, their journey taking them to the farthest reaches of the globe in search of the chosen one who would wield the power of the Object and bring an end to Ms. Gilbert's reign of terror once and for all.

Himalayan Convergence

The towering peaks of the Himalayas loomed before them, their majestic forms reaching towards the heavens like ancient sentinels guarding the secrets of the world. Dr. Geet Adhikary, Professor Bulbul, and Detective Chand Adhikary stood at the foot of the mountains, their resolve unyielding as they prepared to face their most perilous challenge yet.

As they ventured deeper into the heart of the Himalayas, the air grew thin and icy, biting at their skin with a relentless chill. But despite the harsh conditions, they pressed on undeterred, their determination unyielding in the face of the challenges that lay ahead.

Their journey led them through treacherous mountain passes and winding valleys, each step bringing them closer to their destination – a hidden monastery nestled amidst the peaks, rumored to hold the key to unlocking the final mystery of the Object.

As they approached the monastery, they could sense that they were not alone – a sense of unease hung heavy in the air, as if the mountains themselves were watching their every move with keen interest. But Dr. Geet and his companions were undeterred, their hearts set on uncovering the truth no matter what dangers lay in their path.

As they reached the entrance to the monastery, they were greeted by a group of robed monks, their expressions serene but watchful as they regarded the intruders with curiosity. With a sense of reverence, Dr. Geet bowed respectfully to the monks, his hands clasped together in a gesture of humility.

"We seek knowledge," he said, his voice echoing softly through the mountain air. "Knowledge that may hold the key to unlocking the mysteries of the Object."

The head monk regarded Dr. Geet with a knowing gaze, his eyes shining with ancient wisdom as he spoke. "The path to enlightenment is not an easy one, Dr. Adhikary," he said, his voice soft but firm. "But if you seek the truth, then you must prove yourself worthy of it."

With a nod of understanding, Dr. Geet and his companions followed the monks into the depths of the monastery, their hearts pounding with anticipation as they prepared to face whatever trials lay ahead.

Inside the monastery, they were led to a chamber adorned with intricate tapestries and ancient relics, each one a testament to the monastery's rich history and tradition. But it was the object at the center of the chamber – a gleaming artifact bathed in golden light – that drew their attention.

As they approached the artifact, they could feel a sense of power emanating from its surface, as if it were alive with ancient energy. With a sense of reverence, Dr. Geet reached out to touch the artifact, his fingers tingling with anticipation as he made contact with its smooth surface.

Suddenly, a blinding light erupted from the artifact, enveloping Dr. Geet and his companions in its radiant glow. With a sense of awe, they watched as images danced before their eyes – visions of ancient civilizations and lost worlds, each one a piece of the puzzle that would unlock the secrets of the Object.

But their moment of revelation was short-lived, for just as quickly as it had begun, the light faded, leaving them standing in darkness once more. With a sense of wonder, Dr. Geet turned to his companions, his eyes shining with excitement.

"We've found it," he said, his voice filled with awe. "The final piece of the puzzle. The Object's true purpose – to harness the power of the elements and reshape the world according to the will of its wielder."

But their celebration was short-lived, for they knew that their adversary was still out there, lurking in the shadows and waiting for her chance to strike. With a sense of urgency, Dr. Geet and his companions prepared to leave the monastery and confront Ms. Gilbert once and for all.

As they emerged from the monastery, they were greeted by a sight that took their breath away – the mountains stretched out before them in all their glory, their peaks reaching towards the heavens like ancient guardians standing watch over the world below.

But their moment of awe was interrupted by a sudden movement in the shadows – a figure emerging from the darkness with a malevolent gleam in her eyes. It was Ms. Gilbert, their adversary, and she had no intention of letting them escape unscathed.

With a wave of her hand, Ms. Gilbert summoned her minions, and they moved in to surround Dr. Geet and his companions. But the Adhikary family was not about to go down without a fight.

With a battle cry, Chand sprang into action, his fists flying as he engaged Ms. Gilbert's minions in a fierce hand-to-hand combat. Meanwhile, Dr. Geet and Professor Bulbul exchanged knowing glances, their minds racing as they searched for a way to outmaneuver their adversary.

Suddenly, Dr. Geet's eyes lit up with realization as he spotted a series of ancient symbols carved into the mountainside. With a sense of urgency, he motioned for his companions to follow him as he raced towards the symbols, his heart pounding with excitement as he realized their significance.

As they reached the symbols, Dr. Geet began to chant in a language long forgotten, his voice echoing through the mountains like a powerful incantation. With each word, the symbols began to glow with an otherworldly light, illuminating the darkness with their radiant glow.

And then, with a deafening roar, the mountains themselves seemed to come alive, the very earth shaking beneath their feet as ancient guardians emerged from the shadows to confront their adversaries. With a sense of awe, Dr. Geet and his companions watched as the guardians unleashed their fury upon Ms. Gilbert and her minions, their power unmatched by any mortal force.

With their adversary defeated and the Object's true purpose revealed, Dr. Geet and his companions knew that their journey was far from over. But as they stood amidst the towering peaks of the Himalayas, their hearts filled with hope and determination, they knew that they were ready to face whatever challenges lay ahead – together, as a family.

As the dust settled and the echoes of the battle faded into the Himalayan air, Dr. Geet, Professor Bulbul, and Detective Chand stood amidst the towering peaks, their hearts filled with a mixture of relief and determination. The confrontation with Ms. Gilbert had been fierce, but they had emerged victorious, and now they were closer than ever to unraveling the mysteries of the Object.

But even as they caught their breath and surveyed the aftermath of the battle, they knew that their journey was far from over. The Object still held many secrets, and there were forces at work in the world that would stop at nothing to claim its power for themselves.

With a sense of purpose, Dr. Geet turned to his companions, his eyes shining with determination. "We must continue our quest," he said, his voice echoing with conviction. "We cannot rest until we have unlocked the full potential of the Object and ensured that it is used for the good of mankind."

Chand nodded in agreement, his expression grave as he considered the challenges that lay ahead. "But where do we go from here?" he asked, his voice tinged with uncertainty. "The Object's true purpose has been revealed, but there is still much we do not know."

Dr. Geet's mind raced as he pondered Chand's question, his thoughts swirling with possibilities. Suddenly, a spark of inspiration lit up his eyes, and he turned to his companions with newfound resolve.

"We must seek out the guardians of the Object – the ancient beings who have protected it for centuries," he said, his voice filled with excitement. "They alone hold the key to unlocking its full potential and ensuring that it is used wisely."

With a sense of purpose, Dr. Geet and his companions set out once more, their journey taking them deeper into the heart of the Himalayas in search of the guardians of the Object. Along the way, they encountered many challenges and obstacles, from treacherous mountain passes to hidden caves and ancient ruins.

But with each step, their resolve only grew stronger, their determination unyielding in the face of adversity. And finally, after days of arduous travel, they reached their destination – a remote monastery hidden high in the mountains, its ancient stone walls weathered by centuries of wind and snow.

As they approached the monastery, they were greeted by a group of robed monks, their expressions serene but watchful as they regarded the intruders with curiosity. With a sense of reverence, Dr. Geet bowed respectfully to the monks, his hands clasped together in a gesture of humility.

"We seek knowledge," he said, his voice echoing softly through the mountain air. "Knowledge that may hold the key to unlocking the true potential of the Object."

The head monk regarded Dr. Geet with a knowing gaze, his eyes shining with ancient wisdom as he spoke. "The path to enlightenment is not an easy one, Dr. Adhikary," he said, his voice soft but firm. "But if you seek the wisdom of the guardians, then you must prove yourself worthy of their trust."

With a nod of understanding, Dr. Geet and his companions followed the monks into the depths of the monastery, their hearts pounding with anticipation as they prepared to face whatever trials lay ahead. Little did they know, their journey was about to take them to the very heart of the Object's power – and the ultimate showdown with the forces of darkness that sought to claim it for their own.

The Arakan Abyss

Deep within the tangled depths of the Arakan Yoma, Rupert Wallace and Detective Chand Adhikary found themselves ensnared in a deadly game of cat and mouse with their adversaries. Surrounded by dense foliage and hidden dangers, they knew that escape would not come easy.

As they trudged through the thick undergrowth, the air thick with humidity and the sounds of the jungle echoing all around them, Rupert and Chand remained ever vigilant, their senses alert for any sign of danger lurking in the shadows.

Suddenly, a rustling in the bushes ahead sent a jolt of adrenaline coursing through their veins, and they instinctively reached for their weapons, ready to confront whatever threat lay in wait.

But to their surprise, it was not their enemies that emerged from the foliage, but rather a group of local villagers, their faces etched with fear and desperation as they pleaded for help.

"We are trapped," one of the villagers cried, his voice trembling with emotion. "The jungle is alive with danger, and we cannot find our way out. Please, you must help us."

Rupert and Chand exchanged wary glances, their minds racing with possibilities as they considered their options. They knew that helping the villagers would only delay their own escape, but they could not turn a blind eye to those in need.

With a sense of determination, they agreed to aid the villagers in their quest for freedom, their hearts heavy with the knowledge that their own lives hung in the balance.

Together, they ventured deeper into the heart of the jungle, their senses on high alert for any sign of danger lurking in the shadows. But as they pressed on, they soon realized that their enemies were not far behind.

With each passing moment, the jungle seemed to close in around them, its dense foliage and twisting vines creating a labyrinth of obstacles that threatened to ensnare them at every turn.

But Rupert and Chand were not about to go down without a fight. Drawing upon their training and experience, they navigated the treacherous terrain with skill and precision, their minds sharp and their senses honed to a razor's edge.

Suddenly, a group of armed mercenaries emerged from the shadows, their weapons raised and their eyes filled with malice as they closed in on their prey.

With a shout, Rupert and Chand sprang into action, their movements fluid and calculated as they engaged their adversaries in a deadly dance of combat. Bullets flew and blades clashed as they fought tooth and nail for survival, their determination unyielding in the face of overwhelming odds.

But just when it seemed that all hope was lost, a deafening roar echoed through the jungle, shaking the ground beneath their feet and sending their enemies reeling back in fear.

With a sense of awe, Rupert and Chand watched as a massive creature emerged from the foliage, its massive form towering over them like a living nightmare. It was a Bengal tiger, its golden fur shimmering in the dappled sunlight as it prowled through the undergrowth with deadly grace.

Realizing that they were no match for the ferocious beast, Rupert and Chand made a break for it, their hearts pounding with adrenaline as they raced through the jungle with the tiger hot on their heels.

But just as they reached the edge of the jungle, disaster struck – the ground beneath their feet gave way, sending them tumbling into a dark abyss below.

As they plummeted into the depths of the Arakan Yoma, Rupert and Chand braced themselves for impact, their minds racing with the realization that they were trapped with no way out.

But even in the face of certain doom, they refused to give up hope. With their wits and skills pushed to the limit, they knew that their only chance of survival lay in finding a way to escape the clutches of the jungle and make it back to safety.

As they plunged deeper into the darkness, their resolve hardened, their determination unyielding in the face of the perils that lay ahead. For Rupert Wallace and Detective Chand Adhikary, the Arakan Abyss was just another obstacle to overcome on their quest for justice and redemption. And with each passing moment, they drew closer to the ultimate showdown with their enemies – a battle that would test their courage, their strength, and their will to survive.

As Rupert and Chand tumbled into the depths of the Arakan Yoma, darkness enveloped them like a suffocating shroud. The air rushed past them, their hearts pounding with adrenaline as they fell deeper into the unknown abyss.

With no way to control their descent, they braced themselves for the inevitable impact, their minds racing with thoughts of survival. But as they hurtled towards the bottom, a glimmer of hope pierced the darkness – a narrow ledge jutted out from the sheer rock face, offering them a slim chance of escape.

With lightning-fast reflexes, Rupert and Chand reached out, their fingers grasping desperately for purchase as they fought against the pull of gravity. Miraculously, they managed to catch hold of the ledge just in time, their bodies slamming against the unforgiving stone with bone-jarring force.

For a moment, they hung suspended in mid-air, their muscles straining against the weight of their bodies as they struggled to pull themselves to safety. With every ounce of strength they possessed, they hauled themselves up onto the ledge, their chests heaving with exertion as they collapsed onto the solid ground.

As they lay there catching their breath, the enormity of their situation sank in – they were trapped in the depths of the Arakan Yoma, with no way out and their enemies closing in fast. But even in the face of overwhelming odds, they refused to give up hope.

With a sense of determination, they picked themselves up and pressed on, their minds focused on the task at hand. They knew that they had to find a way to escape the abyss and make it back to safety before it was too late.

But as they ventured deeper into the darkness, they soon realized that their ordeal was far from over. The walls of the abyss seemed to close in around them, their narrow ledge giving way to sheer cliffs and treacherous drop-offs that threatened to send them tumbling into the depths below.

With each step, they had to navigate a maze of obstacles and pitfalls, their senses on high alert for any sign of danger lurking in the shadows. But despite the ever-present threat of discovery, they pressed on undeterred, their determination unyielding in the face of adversity.

Suddenly, a shaft of light pierced the darkness, illuminating a narrow passageway that led deeper into the abyss. With a sense of hope, Rupert and Chand followed the light, their hearts pounding with anticipation as they ventured further into the unknown.

But as they rounded a corner, they stumbled upon a grisly sight – the remains of a previous expedition, their bodies torn and mangled beyond recognition. It was a grim reminder of the dangers that lurked in the depths of the Arakan Yoma, and a sobering warning of the fate that awaited them if they did not tread carefully.

With a sense of dread, Rupert and Chand pressed on, their senses heightened as they scanned their surroundings for any sign of danger. But despite their best efforts, they could not shake the feeling that they were being watched – that their every move was being tracked by unseen eyes lurking in the darkness.

As they ventured deeper into the abyss, they encountered more obstacles and challenges, each one more perilous than the last. But with their wits and skills pushed to the limit, they persevered, determined to escape the clutches of the jungle and make it back to safety.

And then, just when it seemed that all hope was lost, they stumbled upon a narrow tunnel carved into the rock, its entrance hidden from view by a thick veil of foliage. With a sense of urgency, they made their way inside, their hearts pounding with anticipation as they ventured further into the unknown.

But as they navigated the winding passageways of the tunnel, they soon realized that they were not alone – their enemies were hot on their trail, their footsteps echoing through the darkness like a death knell.

With no time to spare, Rupert and Chand pushed themselves to their limits, their bodies aching with exhaustion as they raced against the clock to reach the surface before it was too late. For trapped in the depths of the Arakan Yoma, there was no room for error – only the relentless pursuit of survival in a world where danger lurked around every corner.

Temple of Shadows

The ancient temples of Angkor Wat, Bayom, and Angkor Thom rose from the dense jungle like silent sentinels guarding the secrets of centuries past. As Professor Bulbul led the way through the labyrinthine corridors and towering spires, her heart raced with anticipation. She knew that within these sacred walls lay the final piece of the puzzle – the key to unlocking the true power of the Object.

With each step, the air grew heavy with the weight of history, and Professor Bulbul could feel the echoes of the past reverberating through the ancient stone. But she pushed aside her awe and focused on the task at hand, her mind sharp and her senses alert for any sign of danger lurking in the shadows.

As they ventured deeper into the heart of the temple complex, they encountered a series of intricately carved reliefs and statues, each one a testament to the ancient civilization that had once thrived within these hallowed walls. But it was the inscriptions etched into the stone that caught Professor Bulbul's eye – a series of cryptic symbols and glyphs that spoke of a power long forgotten.

With a sense of determination, Professor Bulbul set to work deciphering the ancient language, her fingers tracing the curves and angles of the symbols with practiced precision. With each word she translated, the pieces of the puzzle began to fall into place, revealing a hidden truth that had been lost to the ages.

But as she delved deeper into the mysteries of the temple, Professor Bulbul soon realized that they were not alone. Shadows lurked in the corners of her vision, their presence ominous and foreboding as they watched her every move with malevolent intent.

With a sense of urgency, Professor Bulbul urged her companions to keep moving, their footsteps echoing through the silent halls as they pressed on towards their goal. But no matter how fast they moved, the shadows seemed to follow, their presence growing stronger with each passing moment.

Suddenly, they came upon a chamber bathed in darkness, its entrance guarded by a series of ancient statues that seemed to come to life in the flickering torchlight. With a sense of trepidation, Professor Bulbul led the way inside, her heart pounding with anticipation as she prepared to confront whatever lay in wait.

But as they entered the chamber, they were greeted by a sight that took their breath away – a gleaming artifact bathed in golden light, its surface shimmering with untold power. It was the Object, the final piece of the puzzle that would unlock the secrets of the ancient temples and reveal the true extent of its power.

With a sense of awe, Professor Bulbul approached the artifact, her hands trembling with excitement as she reached out to touch its smooth surface. As her fingers made contact with the Object, a surge of energy coursed through her, filling her with a sense of purpose and determination unlike anything she had ever experienced before.

With newfound clarity, Professor Bulbul turned to her companions, her eyes shining with determination. "We have found it," she said, her voice filled with awe. "The final piece of the puzzle. The Object's true purpose – to harness the power of the ancient temples and reshape the world according to the will of its wielder."

But their moment of triumph was short-lived, for they knew that their adversaries were still out there, lurking in the shadows and waiting for their chance to strike. With a sense of urgency, Professor Bulbul and her companions prepared to leave the temple and confront their enemies head-on.

As they emerged from the chamber, they were greeted by a sight that filled them with dread – the shadows had multiplied, their forms twisting and shifting in the flickering torchlight as they closed in on their prey.

With no time to spare, Professor Bulbul and her companions raced through the silent halls of the temple, their footsteps echoing through the darkness as they fought to reach safety before it was too late. For trapped within the ancient temples of Angkor Wat, Bayom, and Angkor Thom, there was no room for error – only the relentless pursuit of survival in a world where danger lurked around every corner.

As they sprinted through the labyrinthine corridors of the ancient temples, pursued by the encroaching shadows, Professor Bulbul and her companions knew that their only hope lay in reaching the safety of the outside world. With every step, the darkness seemed to close in around them, its oppressive weight bearing down on their shoulders like a suffocating shroud.

But despite the overwhelming odds stacked against them, they refused to give up hope. With their wits and skills honed by years of experience, they navigated the treacherous maze with a determination that bordered on desperation. Every twist and turn brought them closer to freedom, but also closer to the clutches of their relentless pursuers.

As they reached the outer courtyard of the temple complex, they were met with a scene of chaos and destruction. The shadows had gathered in force, their twisted forms writhing and contorting as they prepared to strike. But Professor Bulbul and her companions stood their ground, their resolve unyielding in the face of imminent danger.

With a battle cry, Rupert Wallace and Detective Chand Adhikary sprang into action, their weapons at the ready as they prepared to face their adversaries head-on. Bullets flew and blades clashed as they fought with all their might, their minds focused on the singular goal of survival.

But the shadows were relentless, their numbers seemingly endless as they closed in on their prey. With each passing moment, Professor Bulbul and her companions found themselves pushed to the brink of exhaustion, their bodies aching with the strain of battle.

Just when it seemed that all hope was lost, a blinding light erupted from the heavens, illuminating the courtyard with its radiant glow. With a sense of awe, Professor Bulbul and her companions watched as the shadows recoiled in fear, their twisted forms dissolving into nothingness as they fled from the purity of the light.

As the last of their enemies vanished into the darkness, Professor Bulbul and her companions collapsed to the ground, their bodies spent from the ordeal. But even as they caught their breath and surveyed the aftermath of the battle, they knew that their journey was far from over.

With the Object in their possession and their enemies vanquished, they now had the power to reshape the world according to their will. But with great power came great responsibility, and they knew that they must use their newfound abilities wisely if they were to prevent history from repeating itself.

With a sense of determination, Professor Bulbul and her companions set out once more, their hearts filled with hope and their minds focused on the future. For trapped within the ancient temples of Angkor Wat, Bayom, and Angkor Thom, they had unlocked the true power of the Object – the power to shape the destiny of mankind for generations to come.

The Last Stand

As the sun dipped below the horizon, casting long shadows across the jungle, the Adhikary family prepared for their final stand. With the Object in their possession and their enemies closing in, they knew that their only hope of survival lay in fighting to the bitter end.

With their backs against the wall, Professor Bulbul, Dr. Geet Adhikary, Detective Chand Adhikary, and Rupert Wallace stood side by side, their weapons at the ready as they awaited the inevitable onslaught. They were outnumbered and outgunned, but they refused to give up without a fight.

In the distance, the sound of approaching footsteps echoed through the jungle, signaling the arrival of their enemies. With a sense of grim determination, the Adhikary family braced themselves for the battle to come, their hearts pounding with adrenaline as they prepared to defend what was rightfully theirs.

As the first wave of attackers emerged from the shadows, the Adhikary family sprang into action, their movements fluid and coordinated as they fought tooth and nail for survival. Bullets flew and blades clashed as they engaged their adversaries in a deadly dance of combat, their determination unyielding in the face of overwhelming odds.

But despite their best efforts, the enemy forces continued to advance, their numbers seemingly endless as they closed in on their prey. With each passing moment, the Adhikary family found themselves pushed to the brink of exhaustion, their bodies battered and bruised from the relentless onslaught.

Just when it seemed that all hope was lost, a voice rang out from the darkness – it was Nicole, Barry Warner's wife, held captive by Ms. Gilbert's forces and used as a bargaining chip to lure the Adhikary family into a trap.

With a sense of desperation, the Adhikary family redoubled their efforts, their minds focused on the singular goal of rescuing Nicole from certain doom. With bullets flying and explosions rocking the jungle, they fought their way through the enemy ranks, their determination unyielding in the face of overwhelming odds.

But as they reached Nicole's side, they realized that their ordeal was far from over. Ms. Gilbert herself emerged from the shadows, her eyes blazing with fury as she prepared to strike the final blow.

With a defiant roar, the Adhikary family charged forward, their weapons raised and their hearts filled with courage as they confronted their greatest adversary. Bullets flew and blades clashed as they engaged Ms. Gilbert in a deadly duel, their movements fueled by adrenaline and determination as they fought for their lives.

But even as they battled with all their might, they knew that victory was far from assured. Ms. Gilbert was a formidable opponent, her skills honed by years of training and experience as she fought tooth and nail to defend what she believed to be rightfully hers.

With each passing moment, the Adhikary family found themselves pushed to the brink of exhaustion, their bodies battered and bruised from the relentless onslaught. But they refused to give up, drawing upon their inner strength and resolve as they fought to protect the Object and rescue Nicole from certain doom.

And then, just when it seemed that all hope was lost, a blinding light erupted from the heavens, illuminating the jungle with its radiant glow. With a sense of awe, the Adhikary family watched as the shadows recoiled in fear, their twisted forms dissolving into nothingness as they fled from the purity of the light.

As the last of their enemies vanished into the darkness, the Adhikary family collapsed to the ground, their bodies spent from the ordeal. But even as they caught their breath and surveyed the aftermath of the battle, they knew that their journey was far from over.

With the Object in their possession and Nicole rescued from certain doom, they now had the power to reshape the world according to their will. But with great power came great responsibility, and they knew that they must use their newfound abilities wisely if they were to prevent history from repeating itself.

With a sense of determination, the Adhikary family set out once more, their hearts filled with hope and their minds focused on the future. For trapped within the ancient temples of Angkor Wat, Bayom, and Angkor Thom, they had unlocked the true power of the Object – the power to shape the destiny of mankind for generations to come.

As the adrenaline of the battle began to ebb away, leaving behind a palpable sense of exhaustion, the Adhikary family gathered themselves amidst the wreckage of the jungle. Their breaths came in ragged gasps, chests heaving with the exertion of combat, but their spirits remained resolute.

With the Object now secured and Nicole freed from captivity, they knew their mission was far from over. Though the immediate threat had been vanquished, they were well aware that others would inevitably seek to harness the power of the Object for their own nefarious purposes.

"We cannot afford to rest on our laurels," Dr. Geet Adhikary declared, his voice firm and commanding despite the weariness that weighed upon him. "Our enemies may be vanquished for now, but there will always be others who seek to wield the Object's power for their own ends."

Rupert Wallace nodded in agreement, his eyes scanning the surrounding jungle warily for any sign of movement. "We must remain vigilant," he cautioned. "The shadows may have retreated for now, but they will return, and we must be ready to face them head-on."

With a sense of purpose, the Adhikary family set about regrouping and preparing for the challenges that lay ahead. Though they were physically and emotionally drained from the ordeal they had just endured, their resolve remained unshaken, their determination unwavering in the face of adversity.

As they tended to their wounds and gathered their supplies, they knew that their journey was far from over. With the power of the Object at their disposal, they had the ability to reshape the world and ensure a future free from tyranny and oppression.

But with that power came great responsibility, and they knew that they must use it wisely if they were to prevent history from repeating itself. For trapped within the ancient temples of Angkor Wat, Bayom, and Angkor Thom, they had unlocked the true potential of the Object – the power to shape the destiny of mankind for generations to come.

With a sense of determination, the Adhikary family set out once more into the unknown, their hearts filled with hope and their minds focused on the future. For though their journey had been fraught with danger and uncertainty, they knew that they were not alone – and together, they would overcome whatever challenges lay ahead, and emerge victorious in the face of adversity.

Into the Fire

As the Adhikary family made their way through the dense jungle, their senses on high alert for any sign of danger, they knew that their journey was far from over. With the Object in their possession and their enemies in hot pursuit, they had little time to rest or regroup.

But as they pressed on through the sweltering heat and oppressive humidity, they soon realized that their enemies were closing in fast. With every passing moment, the sound of approaching footsteps grew louder, their presence looming like a dark shadow over the jungle.

With a sense of urgency, Professor Bulbul led the way through the dense undergrowth, her mind racing with thoughts of escape and survival. But even as they pushed forward, they knew that their enemies would stop at nothing to capture the Object and bend its power to their will.

Suddenly, a deafening roar echoed through the jungle, shaking the ground beneath their feet and sending a shiver down their spines. With a sense of dread, the Adhikary family realized that they were nearing the edge of a volcanic crater – a place of unimaginable danger and untold peril.

With no time to spare, they raced towards the crater's edge, their hearts pounding with adrenaline as they prepared to make their daring escape. But as they reached the precipice, they were met with a sight that took their breath away – the mouth of the volcano loomed before them, a swirling maelstrom of fire and brimstone that seemed to stretch into infinity.

With a sense of trepidation, the Adhikary family prepared to make their descent into the heart of the volcano, their minds filled with thoughts of the dangers that awaited them below. But even as they braced themselves for the unknown, they knew that their only chance of survival lay in facing their fears head-on and confronting the darkness that lurked within.

With a leap of faith, they plunged into the fiery abyss, their bodies engulfed in the searing heat of the volcano's molten depths. With every passing moment, the air grew hotter and the flames grew higher, threatening to consume them in a blaze of glory.

But even as they struggled to maintain their composure amidst the inferno, they knew that their journey was far from over. With every step, they drew closer to their final destination – the heart of the volcano, where betrayal and redemption awaited them in equal measure.

As they neared the bottom of the crater, they were met with a sight that took their breath away – a vast chamber carved into the rock, its walls lined with ancient symbols and glyphs that seemed to pulse with an otherworldly energy. It was here, amidst the swirling mists of the volcano's inner sanctum, that their fate would be decided once and for all.

With a sense of determination, the Adhikary family pressed on, their hearts filled with hope and their minds focused on the task at hand. But even as they ventured deeper into the chamber, they knew that danger lurked around every corner, waiting to strike when they least expected it.

Suddenly, a figure emerged from the shadows, their face obscured by the flickering light of the flames. With a sense of dread, the Adhikary family realized that they had been betrayed – their enemy had followed them into the heart of the volcano, intent on capturing the Object and harnessing its power for their own nefarious purposes.

With a defiant roar, Rupert Wallace stepped forward, his eyes blazing with fury as he confronted their adversary head-on. "You will not have the Object," he declared, his voice ringing out through the chamber with unwavering resolve. "We will stop you, no matter the cost."

But their enemy was undeterred, their eyes filled with malice as they prepared to strike the final blow. With a sense of urgency, the Adhikary family sprang into action, their weapons at the ready as they prepared to defend what was rightfully theirs.

Bullets flew and blades clashed as they fought with all their might, their movements fluid and coordinated as they engaged their adversary in a deadly dance of combat. With every blow, they drew closer to victory, their determination unyielding in the face of overwhelming odds.

But even as they fought with all their might, they knew that their enemy was a formidable foe, their skills honed by years of training and experience. With every passing moment, the battle raged on, the flames of the volcano casting long shadows across the chamber as they clashed in a blaze of glory.

And then, just when it seemed that all hope was lost, a blinding light erupted from the depths of the volcano, illuminating the chamber with its radiant glow. With a sense of awe, the Adhikary family watched as the flames receded, revealing the true power of the Object in all its glory.

With a single touch, they harnessed its power, channeling its energy into a devastating wave of light that consumed their enemy in a blinding flash. With a triumphant roar, the Adhikary family emerged victorious, their mission complete and their enemies vanquished once and for all.

As they stood amidst the smoldering ruins of the volcano's inner sanctum, their hearts filled with pride and their minds filled with thoughts of the future, they knew that their journey was far from over. For with the power of the Object at their disposal, they had the ability to reshape the world and ensure a future free from tyranny and oppression.

With a sense of determination, they set out once more into the unknown, their hearts filled with hope and their minds focused on the future. For though their journey had been fraught with danger and uncertainty, they knew that they were not alone.

The Phoenix Rises

As the smoke cleared and the embers of the volcanic crater smoldered around them, Rupert Wallace and the Adhikary family stood amidst the ruins, their bodies battered and bruised, but their spirits unbroken. Despite the betrayal and the chaos that had unfolded within the fiery depths of the volcano, they refused to be deterred. Instead, they saw it as an opportunity – a chance to regroup, to strategize, and to emerge stronger than ever before.

With a sense of determination, Rupert turned to his companions, his eyes ablaze with a fierce resolve. "We may have suffered a setback," he declared, his voice echoing through the charred remains of the chamber, "but we will not be defeated. We will rise from the ashes stronger than ever before, and we will not rest until we have achieved our ultimate goal."

His words resonated with the rest of the Adhikary family, each member nodding in silent agreement. They knew that their journey was far from over – that their enemies still lurked in the shadows, waiting for their chance to strike. But they refused to cower in fear. Instead, they embraced the challenge head-on, ready to confront whatever obstacles lay in their path.

With a renewed sense of purpose, they set about formulating a new plan – one that would allow them to turn the tide of battle in their favor and emerge victorious in the ultimate confrontation. They knew that they would need to rely on their wits, their skills, and their unwavering determination if they were to succeed. But they also knew that they were stronger together than they were apart, and that as long as they stood united, they could overcome any obstacle that stood in their way.

Their plan began to take shape, each member of the Adhikary family contributing their unique talents and expertise to the cause. Professor Bulbul delved into her extensive knowledge of ancient languages and history, searching for clues and insights that could aid them in their quest. Dr. Geet Adhikary utilized his keen intellect and analytical skills to devise strategies and tactics that would outsmart their adversaries at every turn. Detective Chand Adhikary honed his investigative prowess, gathering intelligence and information that would prove invaluable in their battle against the forces of darkness.

As they worked tirelessly to prepare for the ultimate confrontation, they knew that their enemies would not rest. They would need to remain vigilant, to stay one step ahead of their adversaries at all times if they were to emerge victorious. But they were undeterred. They had faced adversity before, and they had emerged stronger for it. They would not falter now, not when they were so close to achieving their ultimate goal.

With their preparations complete, Rupert and the Adhikary family set out once more into the unknown, their hearts filled with hope and their minds focused on the future. For though their journey had been long and arduous, they knew that they were not alone – and together, they would overcome whatever challenges lay ahead, and emerge victorious in the face of adversity.

As they ventured into the unknown, their spirits soared with anticipation, their determination unwavering in the face of uncertainty. For trapped within the fiery depths of the volcano, they had risen from the ashes stronger than ever before – ready to face whatever challenges lay ahead, and to emerge victorious in the ultimate confrontation that awaited them.

Shadows of the Past

As Rupert Wallace and the Adhikary family pressed on with their mission, a shadow of unease lingered over them. Secrets from Rupert's past haunted his every step, threatening to unravel the fragile alliance they had forged in their quest to protect the Object.

It was during a moment of respite, as they rested in a secluded safehouse deep in the heart of the jungle, that the truth began to emerge. Rupert sat alone, his thoughts consumed by memories long buried and secrets best left forgotten.

Detective Chand Adhikary approached him cautiously, sensing the weight of guilt and regret that hung heavy in the air. "Rupert," he began, his voice soft and measured, "there's something you need to tell us. Something about your connection to the Object."

Rupert's eyes darkened with a mixture of fear and apprehension as he met Chand's gaze. He knew that the time had come to confront the shadows of his past – to reveal the truth and face the consequences of his actions.

Taking a deep breath, Rupert began to speak, his words halting at first as he struggled to find the right way to explain. "Many years ago," he began, his voice barely above a whisper, "I was a different man. I was consumed by ambition, driven by a desire for power and control."

He recounted the events that had led him to the Object – a relic of untold power that had the ability to reshape the world according to the will of its wielder. He had sought it out, driven by a thirst for knowledge and a hunger for power that had blinded him to the consequences of his actions.

But in his quest to possess the Object, he had unwittingly unleashed forces beyond his control – forces that had threatened to tear the world apart in their relentless pursuit of power. It was only through the intervention of the Adhikary family that he had been saved from the brink of destruction, and he owed them a debt of gratitude that could never be repaid.

As Rupert's tale unfolded, the Adhikary family listened in stunned silence, their minds reeling with the enormity of what he had revealed. They had known Rupert as a trusted ally, a stalwart companion in their quest to protect the Object, but they had never suspected the depths of his connection to it – or the lengths he had gone to protect it.

But even as they grappled with the implications of Rupert's confession, they knew that their mission was far from over. The shadows of the past may have haunted them, but they refused to be defined by them. Together, they would confront whatever challenges lay ahead, and emerge victorious in the face of adversity.

As they ventured deeper into the heart of the jungle, the weight of Rupert's revelation hung heavy in the air, casting a pall over their journey. Each step forward felt like a step into the unknown, the shadows of the past trailing behind them like specters in the night.

But despite the turmoil that churned within them, the Adhikary family remained steadfast in their resolve. They knew that they could not afford to dwell on the past – not when their mission to protect the Object still hung in the balance.

With each passing day, their determination grew stronger, fueled by the knowledge that they were fighting for something greater than themselves. They had seen the devastation that the Object could unleash in the wrong hands, and they were determined to prevent history from repeating itself.

But as they delved deeper into the jungle, they soon realized that their enemies were not far behind. Shadows lurked in every corner, their presence a constant reminder of the dangers that surrounded them.

It was during one such encounter that they were ambushed by a group of mercenaries, their guns blazing as they descended upon the Adhikary family with ruthless efficiency. Caught off guard, Rupert and his companions fought tooth and nail to defend themselves, their weapons flashing in the darkness as they engaged their adversaries in a deadly dance of combat.

But even as they fought with all their might, they soon found themselves outnumbered and outgunned, their backs against the wall as the mercenaries closed in for the kill. With each passing moment, the situation grew more dire, their chances of survival dwindling with every breath.

Just when it seemed that all hope was lost, a familiar face emerged from the shadows – Barry Warner, the man whose betrayal had set their journey into motion. With a sense of desperation, he threw himself into the fray, his guns blazing as he fought alongside Rupert and the Adhikary family to fend off their attackers.

Though their alliance was tenuous at best, they knew that they had no choice but to work together if they were to survive. With Barry's help, they were able to turn the tide of battle, driving back their enemies with a ferocity born of desperation.

The Final Gambit

As the Adhikary family and their unlikely ally, Barry Warner, continued their journey through the dense jungle, their thoughts turned to their ultimate goal: to secure the Object and prevent it from falling into the wrong hands. With each step forward, the weight of their mission pressed upon them, driving them ever closer to the moment of reckoning.

Their path led them to a remote stronghold nestled deep within the heart of the jungle – the lair of Ms. Gilbert, their most formidable adversary yet. It was here that the Object lay hidden, its power waiting to be unleashed upon the world.

With a sense of determination, Rupert Wallace and the Adhikary family prepared to launch their final assault, their hearts filled with hope and their minds focused on the task at hand. They knew that they were risking everything in their quest to secure the Object once and for all, but they refused to back down in the face of adversity.

As they approached the stronghold, they were met with a wall of resistance – Ms. Gilbert's forces were ready and waiting, their guns trained on the intruders as they prepared to defend their territory at all costs. But the Adhikary family was undeterred. With Barry Warner at their side, they launched their assault with a ferocity born of desperation, their weapons flashing in the darkness as they fought tooth and nail to overcome their enemies.

Bullets flew and blades clashed as they battled their way through the stronghold, their movements swift and coordinated as they pressed forward with unwavering resolve. With each passing moment, they drew closer to their goal, their determination unyielding in the face of overwhelming odds.

But even as they fought with all their might, they soon realized that their enemy was not going to go down without a fight. Ms. Gilbert herself emerged from the shadows, her eyes blazing with fury as she prepared to strike the final blow.

With a defiant roar, Rupert Wallace stepped forward, his gaze locked with Ms. Gilbert's as he prepared to confront her head-on. "You will not win," he declared, his voice ringing out through the stronghold with unwavering resolve. "We will stop you, no matter the cost."

But Ms. Gilbert was undeterred, her lips curling into a sinister smile as she prepared to unleash her ultimate weapon – the power of the Object itself. With a wave of her hand, she summoned forth a wave of energy that threatened to consume everything in its path, leaving destruction in its wake.

With a sense of urgency, the Adhikary family sprang into action, their minds racing as they searched for a way to stop Ms. Gilbert and prevent her from unleashing the full power of the Object. With each passing moment, the stakes grew higher, their chances of success dwindling with every breath.

But even as they faced seemingly insurmountable odds, they refused to give up hope. With Barry Warner at their side, they launched a daring gambit to disrupt Ms. Gilbert's plans and secure the Object once and for all.

With a swift and decisive maneuver, they managed to disable Ms. Gilbert's control over the Object, leaving her powerless and vulnerable in the face of their onslaught. With a triumphant roar, they launched their final assault, their weapons flashing in the darkness as they fought tooth and nail to overcome their adversary.

In the end, it was their unwavering determination and their refusal to back down in the face of adversity that proved to be their greatest weapon. With a final blow, they defeated Ms. Gilbert once and for all, securing the Object and preventing it from falling into the wrong hands.

With Ms. Gilbert's stronghold now in ruins and the Object secured, the Adhikary family and Barry Warner breathed a collective sigh of relief. Yet, their victory was tinged with the knowledge that their enemies would not rest until they had the Object in their possession.

As they regrouped amidst the wreckage of the stronghold, Rupert Wallace's gaze swept over his companions, a mixture of exhaustion and determination etched on their faces. "We cannot afford to let our guard down," he said, his voice grave. "Our enemies will not stop until they have what they seek. We must remain vigilant."

The Adhikary family nodded in agreement, their resolve unwavering. They knew that their journey was far from over, and that they would need to stay one step ahead of their adversaries if they were to succeed.

With the Object secured, their next challenge lay in finding a safe place to keep it hidden from those who would seek to exploit its power. Dr. Geet Adhikary suggested a remote temple hidden deep within the jungle, a place of ancient power that few knew existed.

With their destination set, the Adhikary family and Barry Warner set out once more into the jungle, their hearts filled with hope and their minds focused on the task at hand. They knew that the journey would not be easy, but they were determined to see it through to the end.

As they traveled deeper into the jungle, they encountered new challenges at every turn. From treacherous terrain to hostile wildlife, their path was fraught with danger. But with each obstacle they faced, they grew stronger, their bond as a family growing ever stronger with each passing moment.

Finally, after days of arduous travel, they arrived at their destination – the remote temple hidden deep within the jungle. As they approached, they were struck by the sense of ancient power that permeated the air, a feeling of reverence and awe that washed over them like a tidal wave.

With a sense of purpose, they made their way inside the temple, their footsteps echoing through the hallowed halls as they searched for a suitable resting place for the Object. Eventually, they came upon a hidden chamber deep within the heart of the temple, a place of unparalleled beauty and serenity.

With great care, they placed the Object within the chamber, its power contained within the confines of the temple's ancient walls. As they stepped back, they knew that they had done what needed to be done – the Object was safe, at least for now.

But even as they celebrated their victory, they knew that their journey was far from over. With their enemies still out there, lurking in the shadows, they knew that they would need to remain vigilant if they were to protect the Object and ensure a future free from tyranny and oppression.

The Object Revealed

The remote temple hidden deep within the jungle stood silent and still, its ancient walls shrouded in mystery and intrigue. Inside, the Adhikary family and Barry Warner gathered around the Object, their eyes drawn to its shimmering surface with a mixture of awe and trepidation.

For days, they had journeyed through the jungle, facing untold dangers and overcoming countless obstacles in their quest to protect the Object. Now, as they stood before it, they could feel the weight of its power pressing upon them, a palpable presence that seemed to emanate from within.

As they gazed upon the Object, a sense of anticipation filled the air, their hearts racing with excitement and uncertainty. They knew that the true nature of its power had yet to be revealed, and they braced themselves for whatever revelations lay ahead.

With a sense of trepidation, Dr. Geet Adhikary reached out and touched the Object, his fingers tracing its intricate patterns with reverence. As he did, a surge of energy coursed through him, filling him with a sense of clarity and purpose.

Suddenly, images began to flash before his eyes – visions of distant lands and forgotten civilizations, of battles fought and victories won. He saw the Object's true power, its ability to shape the world according to the desires of its wielder.

But as the visions continued, Dr. Geet's expression darkened, his eyes filled with a mixture of fear and uncertainty. He saw the potential for destruction that lay within the Object, the temptation to use its power for selfish gain and personal glory.

With a sense of urgency, he pulled away from the Object, his heart heavy with the weight of what he had seen. "We cannot allow the Object to fall into the wrong hands," he said, his voice grave. "Its power is too great, too dangerous to be wielded by mere mortals."

The rest of the Adhikary family nodded in agreement, their minds racing with thoughts of the responsibility that lay before them. They knew that they could not simply leave the Object hidden away in the temple, where it could be discovered by those who sought to exploit its power for their own nefarious purposes.

With a sense of determination, Rupert Wallace stepped forward, his gaze locked with the Object as he prepared to confront its power head-on. "We must destroy it," he declared, his voice ringing out through the temple with unwavering resolve. "We cannot allow it to bring harm to the world."

But even as he spoke, a sense of doubt crept into his mind, a nagging voice that whispered of the Object's potential for greatness. He knew that destroying it would mean sacrificing its power – and with it, the chance to reshape the world according to his own desires.

As the Adhikary family and Barry Warner debated their next course of action, a sense of tension hung heavy in the air, their conflicting beliefs and desires threatening to tear them apart. But in the end, they knew that they had to make a choice – to destroy the Object and risk losing its power forever, or to keep it safe and risk the consequences of its potential for destruction.

With a heavy heart, they made their decision. Together, they vowed to keep the Object hidden away, where it could do no harm to the world. And as they left the temple behind, their minds filled with thoughts of the future, they knew that they had made the right choice – for themselves, and for the world they had sworn to protect.

As they emerged from the temple, the Adhikary family and Barry Warner felt a weight lift from their shoulders. Their decision to keep the Object hidden away, away from those who would seek to exploit its power, brought a sense of relief and purpose to their mission.

But even as they made their way through the jungle, their minds were haunted by the memories of the Object's power and the visions it had revealed. They knew that they could not simply forget what they had seen, nor could they ignore the responsibility that had been thrust upon them.

As they traveled, they encountered new challenges and obstacles, each one testing their resolve and their bond as a family. From treacherous terrain to hostile wildlife, their journey was fraught with danger at every turn.

But with each challenge they faced, they grew stronger, their determination unwavering in the face of adversity. They knew that their mission was far from over, and that they would need to remain vigilant if they were to protect the Object and ensure a future free from tyranny and oppression.

As they traveled, they encountered new allies and enemies alike, each one adding to the complexity of their journey. From rogue agents to ancient guardians, they faced a myriad of threats that tested their skills and their resolve.

But through it all, they remained united, their bond as a family stronger than ever before. Together, they faced each new challenge head-on, their determination unwavering in the face of adversity.

Eventually, they emerged from the jungle, their journey coming to an end as they returned to the safety of their home in South Kolkata. But even as they settled back into their lives, they knew that their mission was far from over.

For though the Object was hidden away, its power still lingered, a constant reminder of the dangers that lay ahead. And as long as there were those who sought to exploit its power, the Adhikary family knew that they would need to remain vigilant, ready to confront whatever challenges lay ahead.

But for now, they allowed themselves a moment of respite, a chance to rest and recuperate after their long and arduous journey.

Shadows of Redemption

In the aftermath of their harrowing journey to protect the Object, the Adhikary family found themselves back in the safety of their home in South Kolkata. Yet, despite the tranquility of their surroundings, the memories of their adventure still lingered in their minds, a constant reminder of the dangers they had faced and the sacrifices they had made along the way.

As they gathered together in the comfort of their lavish home, a sense of camaraderie filled the air, their bond as a family stronger than ever before. But beneath the surface, there lingered a sense of unease, a nagging doubt that whispered of the challenges still to come.

Dr. Geet Adhikary sat in silence, his thoughts consumed by the events of their journey and the sacrifices they had made along the way. He knew that their mission had been a success – the Object was hidden away, safe from those who would seek to exploit its power for their own gain. But at what cost?

As he reflected on their journey, Dr. Geet couldn't help but feel a sense of guilt weighing heavily on his heart. He had led his family into danger, risking their lives in pursuit of a cause that seemed to grow more uncertain with each passing day. And though they had emerged victorious, he knew that the scars of their journey would linger long after the dust had settled.

Across the room, Professor Bulbul sat quietly, her eyes filled with a mixture of sorrow and determination. She had always been the rock of the family, the one who held them together in times of trouble. But even she couldn't deny the toll that their journey had taken on them all.

As she looked around at her family, she couldn't help but feel a sense of pride in all that they had accomplished. Despite the odds stacked against them, they had remained united, their bond as a family stronger than ever before. And though the road ahead was uncertain, she knew that they would face it together, as they always had.

Detective Chand Adhikary paced back and forth, his mind racing with thoughts of their journey and the challenges that lay ahead. He had always been the protector of the family, the one who stood on the front lines in defense of those he loved. But even he couldn't shake the feeling of doubt that gnawed at him from within.

As he grappled with his thoughts, Detective Chand couldn't help but feel a sense of responsibility weighing heavily on his shoulders. He had sworn to protect his family at all costs, yet he couldn't shake the feeling that he had failed them in some way. And though they had emerged from their journey relatively unscathed, he knew that the scars ran deeper than any physical wound could ever reach.

Finally, Rupert Wallace broke the silence, his voice cutting through the tension like a knife. "We may have emerged victorious from our journey," he began, his eyes meeting those of each member of the family in turn, "but our work is far from over. The Object may be hidden away for now, but there are still those who would seek to exploit its power for their own gain. We must remain vigilant, ready to confront whatever challenges lie ahead."

His words struck a chord with the rest of the family, their resolve strengthened by his unwavering determination. They knew that their journey was far from over, and that they would need to remain united if they were to overcome whatever challenges lay ahead.

And so, as they sat together in the comfort of their home, the Adhikary family reflected on their journey and the sacrifices they had made along the way. Though the road ahead was uncertain, they knew that they would face it together, as they always had – a family bound by love, loyalty, and the unshakeable belief that no matter how dark the shadows may be, redemption is always within reach.

As the Adhikary family continued their reflection, a sense of determination settled over them like a comforting shroud. They had weathered the storm together, facing the darkest of shadows and emerging stronger for it. Now, as they looked to the future, they knew that their bond as a family would see them through whatever trials lay ahead.

In the quiet of their home, they began to share their thoughts and feelings, each member opening up about their experiences and the lessons they had learned along the way. Dr. Geet spoke of the importance of humility and the dangers of unchecked ambition, his words a cautionary tale born from the mistakes of his past.

Professor Bulbul shared her insights into the power of compassion and empathy, reminding her family of the importance of standing together in times of trouble. She spoke of the strength that came from unity, and the resilience that could be found in the face of adversity.

Detective Chand recounted the challenges he had faced and the sacrifices he had made in defense of his family. He spoke of the moments of doubt and uncertainty that had plagued him, and the strength he had found in the love and support of those he held dear.

And Rupert Wallace, ever the stoic leader, spoke of the importance of perseverance and resilience in the face of adversity. He reminded his family that their journey was far from over, and that they would need to remain vigilant if they were to protect the Object and ensure a future free from tyranny and oppression.

As they spoke, a sense of solidarity settled over the Adhikary family, their bond stronger than ever before. They knew that they would face whatever challenges lay ahead together, united in their determination to protect what was most important to them.

But even as they looked to the future with hope and determination, they knew that the shadows of their past would always linger, a constant reminder of the trials they had faced and the sacrifices they had made along the way.

Yet, in the midst of those shadows, they found redemption – not in the defeat of their enemies or the triumph of their cause, but in the bonds of love and loyalty that held them together as a family. And as they looked ahead to the uncertain future, they knew that no matter what lay in store, they would face it together, as they always had – a family united in purpose and bound by the unbreakable ties of blood and love.

Don't miss out!

Visit the website below and you can sign up to receive emails whenever Walter Wayne publishes a new book. There's no charge and no obligation.

https://books2read.com/r/B-A-NRJTB-GWUUD

BOOKS 2 READ

Connecting independent readers to independent writers.

Also by Walter Wayne

The Scotland Yard Cases
Investigating Alone

The Wallace-Adhikary Spy-Thrillers
The Impenetrable Nexus
Treasure of the Jamaican Buccaneers
Diamonds Aren't Forever
Diamonds In The Shadow
Blood Diamonds
Double Crossed
The Mafia Chronicles
Conspiracy of Chaos
Shadows Of The Lost Empire

About the Author

Walter Wayne is a spy thriller author with decades of experience in intelligence and special operations. He infuses his stories with authentic tradecraft and geopolitical insight, celebrating the courage and resourcefulness of agents and allies to expose truth. He continues consulting for select security agencies while crafting his next book and enjoys raising funds for veterans charities and youth outreach programs.

Milton Keynes UK
Ingram Content Group UK Ltd.
UKHW030755040824
446326UK00015B/53